I Can Rea

PADDiNGTON 2
Paddington's Family and Friends

Adapted by Thomas Macri
Based on Paddington Bear created by Michael Bond

HARPER
An Imprint of HarperCollins Publishers

Dear Parent:
Your child's love of reading starts here!

Every child learns to read in a different way and at his or her own speed. Some go back and forth between reading levels and read favorite books again and again. Others read through each level in order. You can help your young reader improve and become more confident by encouraging his or her own interests and abilities. From books your child reads with you to the first books he or she reads alone, there are I Can Read Books for every stage of reading:

SHARED READING
Basic language, word repetition, and whimsical illustrations, ideal for sharing with your emergent reader

BEGINNING READING
Short sentences, familiar words, and simple concepts for children eager to read on their own

READING WITH HELP
Engaging stories, longer sentences, and language play for developing readers

READING ALONE
Complex plots, challenging vocabulary, and high-interest topics for the independent reader

ADVANCED READING
Short paragraphs, chapters, and exciting themes for the perfect bridge to chapter books

I Can Read Books have introduced children to the joy of reading since 1957. Featuring award-winning authors and illustrators and a fabulous cast of beloved characters, I Can Read Books set the standard for beginning readers.

A lifetime of discovery begins with the magical words "I Can Read!"

Visit www.icanread.com for information
on enriching your child's reading experience.

PADDINGTON™ 2

Paddington's Family and Friends

I Can Read Book® is a trademark of HarperCollins Publishers.

Paddington 2: Paddington's Family and Friends
Based on Paddington Bear created by Michael Bond
Paddington Bear™, Paddington™ and PB™ are trademarks of Paddington and Company Limited. Licensed on
behalf of Studiocanal S.A.S. by Copyrights Group
© Paddington and Company Limited/STUDIOCANAL S.A.S. 2017
All rights reserved. Printed in the United States of America.
No part of this book may be used or reproduced in any manner whatsoever without written permission except
in the case of brief quotations embodied in critical articles and reviews. For information address HarperCollins
Children's Books, a division of HarperCollins Publishers, 195 Broadway, New York, NY 10007.
www.icanread.com

ISBN 978-0-06-282441-7

17 18 19 20 21   LSCC   10 9 8 7 6 5 4 3 2 1   ❖   First Edition

This is Paddington.

He was born in Peru.

He lived there with

his aunt and uncle.

7

Paddington's Aunt Lucy

sent him to live in London.

He stowed away
in a ship's lifeboat.
The ship sailed to England.

He soon found himself
in a train station.
The station was called
Paddington Station.

At the station, Paddington met
his first friends in London.

They are a family
called the Browns.
There are four of them:
mother, father, son, and daughter.

Mr. Brown used to be very serious.
Now he does yoga and drinks
healthy green juices.

Mrs. Brown is an artist.

She is very creative.

She also likes to swim

long distances.

The Browns' daughter is named Judy.

She is kind and smart.

Paddington helped her print

her own newspaper.

The youngest member of the Brown

family is Jonathan.

He is trying to be a famous DJ.

But he also loves old steam trains.

Mrs. Bird is the Browns'
housekeeper.
She is a great friend.
She makes marmalade
with Paddington.

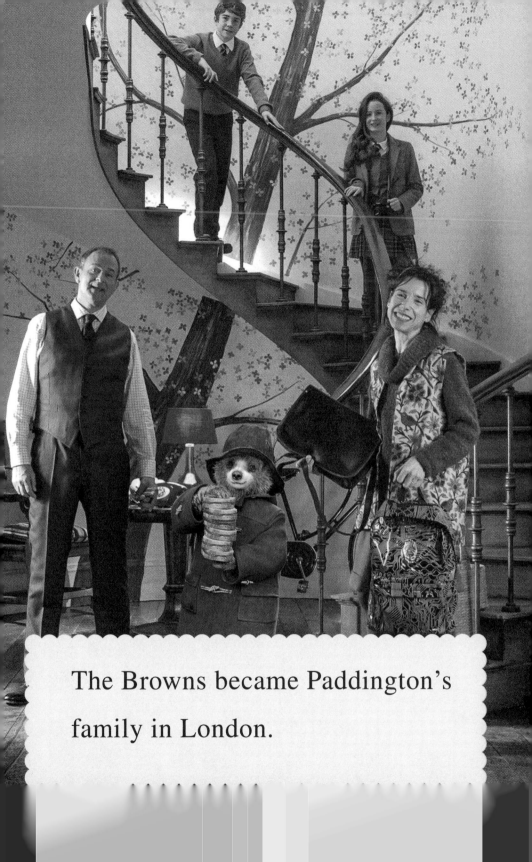

The Browns became Paddington's family in London.

Mr. Gruber is also
Paddington's friend.

He owns an antique shop.

He helped Paddington find a book
to send to his Aunt Lucy in Peru.
The book was all about London.

The pages showed little scenes.
London seemed to come
to life.

Paddington met Phoenix Buchanan
at a world-famous fair.

He was an actor.

He was very interested in

Paddington's book.

Phoenix used to be famous.

Now he just stars

in dog food commercials.

He turns out to be not very nice!
Phoenix blames Paddington
for something he didn't do!

Thankfully the truth comes out.

And Phoenix has to go to jail!

Everyone is happy
for Paddington.
His friends know that he
is kind and curious.

Anybody who knows him
knows this is true!

London is filled with many wonderful people and places. Paddington hopes Aunt Lucy will see them all someday.

Until then, Paddington
is happy to know he
has friends and family
who will always help him!

32